Coral

Molly Idle

L B

Little, Brown and Company
New York Boston

*I*n the sunlight, in the sea, three mermaids made their home. Coral created the reef itself.

Filly looked after the little fish that found food and shelter there.

Manta raised the sharks and rays that fed upon
the fish, keeping the reef in balance.

And so their home was whole and well
while each one shared their part.

But one day, as Coral made her way among
the cays, she came upon an empty hollow,
hidden in the very heart of the reef.

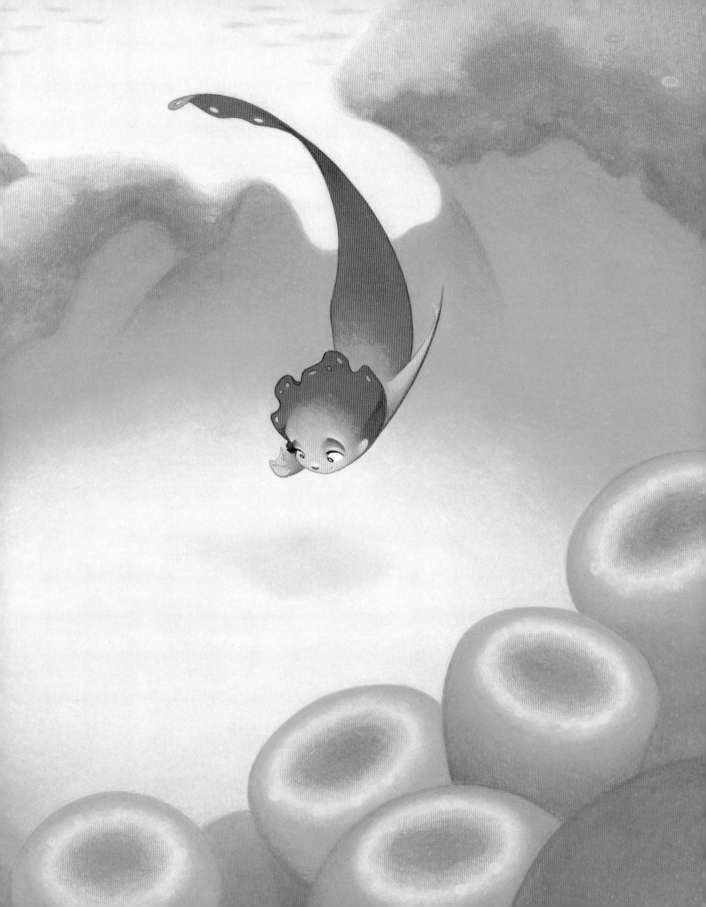

And as she sheltered there from the busy
shoals above, an idea took root with Coral.
She began to think that she should keep
this haven for her very own.

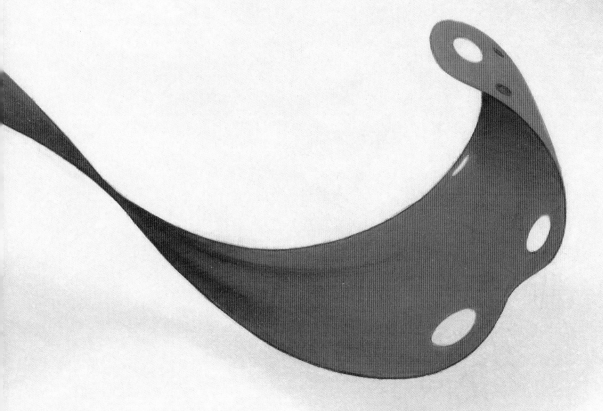

No nibbling fish. No rushing rays.
Just the sunlight, and the sea, and Coral.

So when Filly found her settled there,
Coral's face grew pale—for in her heart,
she did not wish to share.

Then close on Filly's tail came Manta, stirring up a cloud of sand—
and Coral's temper too.

Filling up with white-hot anger, Coral cried, "Enough!"

"You've ruined everything!" she shouted. "I don't want you here."
"But there's room enough for all of us," said Filly as she shied away.
Manta moved to side with her. "We make our home here too."
"I make the reef," Coral countered. "All you make is a mess!"

Her heated words broke over them in waves, driving Filly and Manta from the heart of the reef.

Coral planted herself stubbornly back in place.

But all that grew in the wake of her anger was a feeling of regret.

No nibbling fish. No rushing rays.
Just the sunlight and the sea.

Coral knew then that it was she, and she alone,
who had ruined everything.

And that, alone, she could not set it right.

Reaching out to Filly and Manta,
Coral called, "Please wait! I can make
the reef, but I cannot make it a home…

…without you."

"It takes all of us."

Joining hands, they shared a smile.

So it was that Coral, and Filly, and Manta returned to
the heart of the reef.

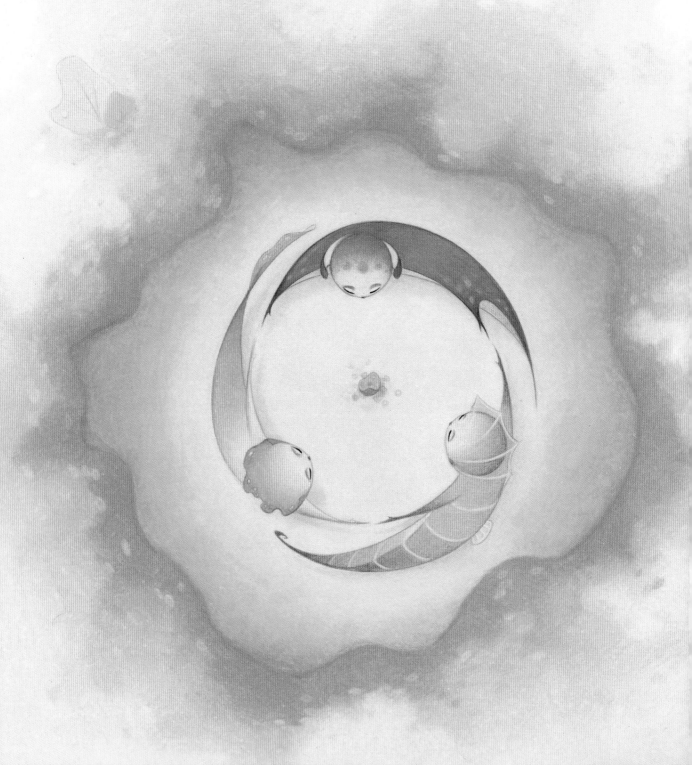

And in the sunlight, in the sea,
three mermaids made their home…

...together.

For all of us

ABOUT THIS BOOK

The illustrations for this book were created with Prismacolor pencils on vellum-finished Bristol. This book was edited by Andrea Spooner and designed by Saho Fujii. The production was supervised by Erika Schwartz, and the production editor was Jen Graham. The text was set in Mrs Eaves, and the display type was hand-lettered by Frances MacLeod.